ROMAN NUMERALS I to MM

NUMERABILIA ROMANA UNO AD DUO MILA

LIBER DE DIFFICILLIMO COMPUTANDO NUMERUM

Arthur Geisert

Houghton Mifflin Company Boston

For art teachers

Gerald Brommer, *age* LXIX

    and

Reinhold Marxhausen, *age* LXXIV

Library of Congress Cataloging-in-Publication Data

Geisert, Arthur.
   Roman numerals I to MM = Numerabilia romana uno ad duo mila /
Arthur Geisert
      p.   cm.
   Summary: Introduces Roman numerals, and by counting pigs in the
illustrations the reader can reinforce the mathematical concept.
   ISBN 0-395-74519-5 (hardcover)
   1. Roman numerals—Juvenile literature.   2. Counting—Juvenile
literature. [1. Roman numerals. 2. Counting.] I. Title.
OA141.3.G45   1996
513.5'5'0148—dc20   95-36247
                                         CIP
                                         AC

For information about this and other Houghton Mifflin trade and
reference books and multimedia products, visit The Bookstore on
the World Wide Web at http://www.hmco.com/trade/.
Printed in the United States of America
HOR 10 9 8 7 6 5 4 3 2

Walter Lorraine 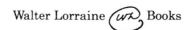 Books

NUMERABILIA ROMANA UNO AD DUO MILA

LIBER DE DIFFICILLIMO COMPUTANDO NUMERUM

Seven letters stand for numbers called Roman numerals. Used alone or in various combinations, they will make every number. The letters are: I, V, X, L, C, D, and M.

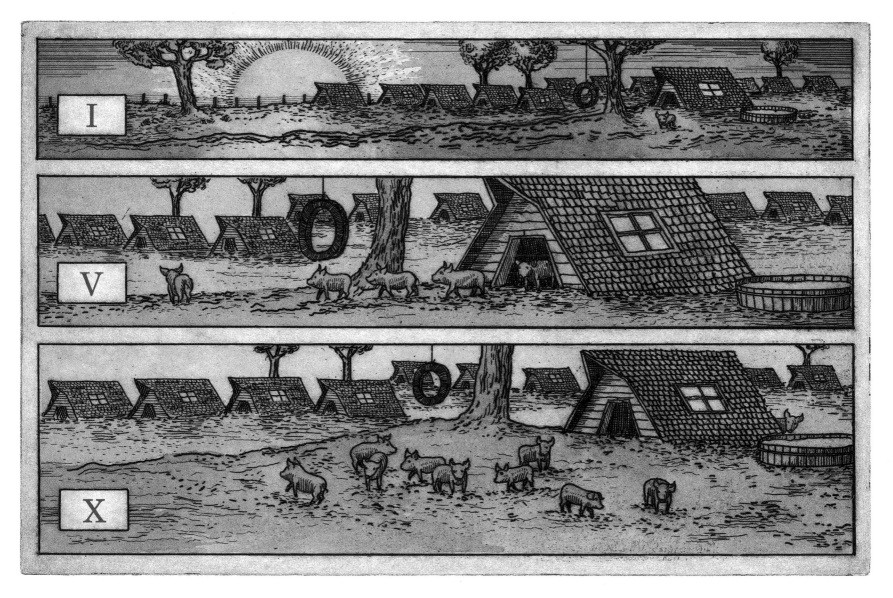

Count the number of pigs to find the value of each numeral.

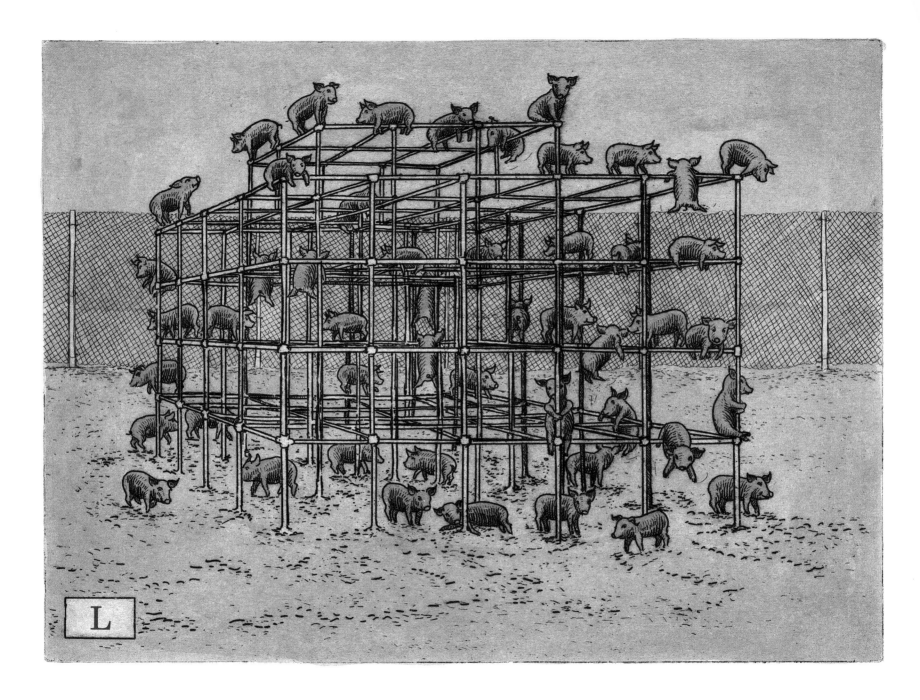

L

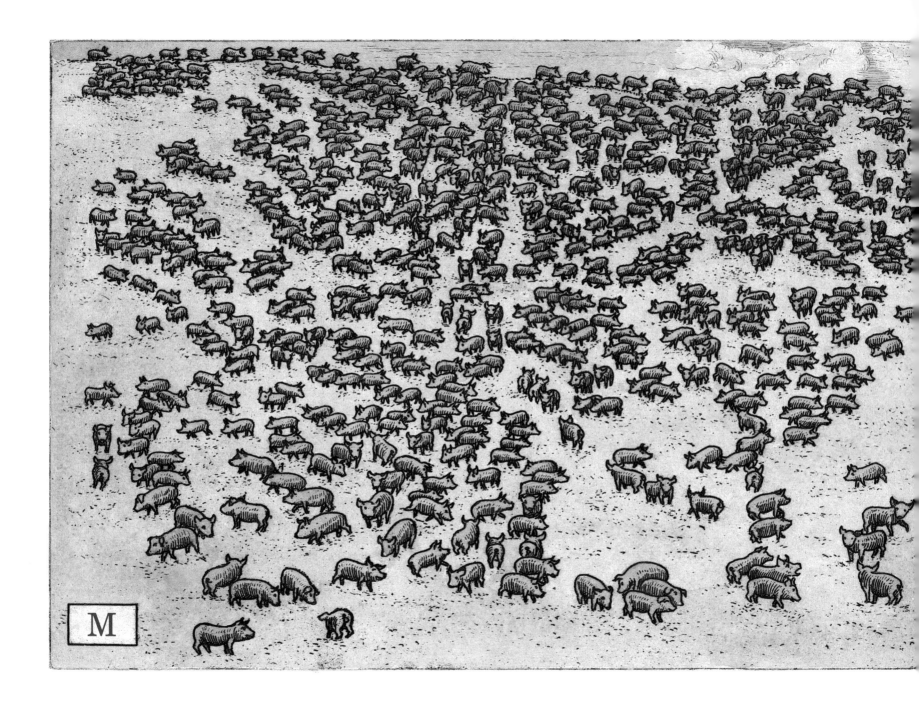

Roman numerals are written and read from left to right. If
numerals of equal value are placed side by side, they are added.
I, X, and C may be used two and three times in a row.

V, L, and D are not used in a row because, when added, they
total an existing numeral. VV=X, so X is used instead.
Likewise, LL=C and DD=M.

MM

M is the largest Roman numeral. It may also be used two and
three times in a row, as may I, X, and C. However, unlike I, X, and C,
M may be repeated many times.

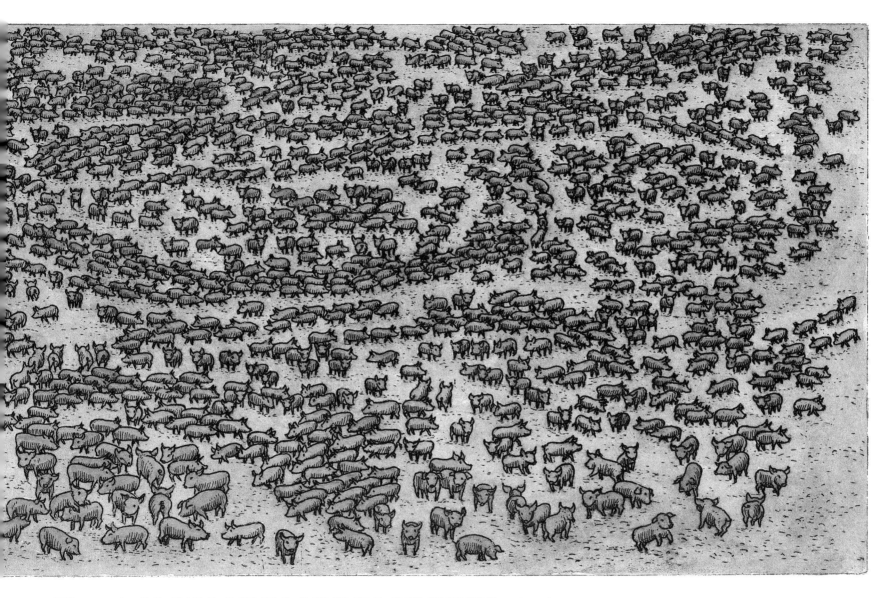

There is M, MM, MMM, MMMM, MMMMM, etcetera.

Numbers are made by adding and subtracting. When writing
a Roman numeral, the largest numeral is written first, followed by
numerals of equal or lesser value.

These numerals are added. However, when a smaller numeral
appears before a larger numeral, it is subtracted from
that numeral. IV and IX are examples.

Numerals that involve subtraction always have a four or nine in that number. XIV and XIX are examples.

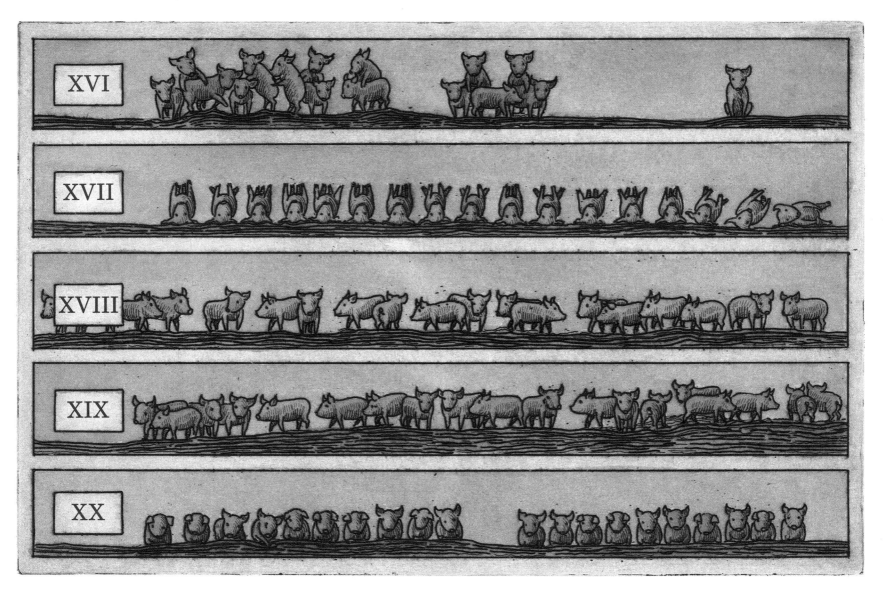

In a long number, subtraction may take place more than once.
This often happens in dates. MCMXC, nineteen ninety, is an example.

The best way to learn Roman numerals is to use them.
If you don't know what the numerals listed are,
count the objects in the picture to find out.

X	Pig Houses	V	Cows
III	Tractors	XI	Evergreen trees
IV	Water tanks	IX	Storage bins

II Tire swings   VII Clouds

 I Eighteen Twelve   IV Birds

X Sandbags   IV Hands

I Nineteen Twenty-two   II Eagles
IX Flowerpots   I Sixteen Twenty
XVI Gopher holes   XX Chain links

I	Eighteen Sixty-one	III	Trash cans
I	Nineteen Five	VL	Pigs
IV	Stone posts	I	Seventeen Fifty

XVIII	Bottles		I	Eighteen Ninety
I	Seventeen Sixty-six		LIV	Boiler bolts
IV	Brown jugs		XIII	Bricks

V   Saw blades   XXXVI   Pigs

I   Nineteen Hundred   I   Nineteen Forty-one

III   Urns   VI   Birds

This Book Contains

XII	Stumps	V	Barrels
XXXII	Pages	II	Mice
VII	Tire swings	IX	Cannonballs
III	Weathervanes	V	Pig statues
XXVI	Birds	II	Sundials
I	Bell	VII	Cows

MMMMDCCCLXIV Pigs